MERLIN

GRAHAM HOWELLS

PONT

In a deep, dark place under the earth,
ancient magic stirred. A wizard was waking.

Arty was hiding from Morgan, the school bully, in a gorse bush. The whole class had come up this hill outside Carmarthen to learn about Merlin the wizard, but instead, Arty was learning about prickles in his bottom.

'Come out for a bashing, Smarty Arty!' called Morgan. Morgan had been the first to call him Arty, and the name had stuck.

Carefully, quietly, Arty crawled backwards through the bush, and found himself in a small clearing. Feeling safer, he sat against an ancient standing stone and breathed more easily. His watch said ten o'clock. He couldn't hide here forever; Mr. Jenkins would wonder where he was.

'Hoy there, boy!' bellowed a voice from very nearby.

Sitting up straight with a jump, Arty banged his head against the stone. He looked around to see an old man with a long white beard, dressed in what seemed to be a very dusty old frock.

'Fear not,' said the old man. 'I see you are a nervous child.'

Arty thought that being scared silly by a weird tramp with a big stick would make anyone nervous.

'You're not the farmer, are you?' said Arty, getting up.

'Farmer? Farmer!' spluttered the old man. 'I am not a tiller of the soil! I am a counsellor of kings! I am the great wizard, Merlin!'

Uh-oh, thought Arty. He could run faster than the old man, and was about to prove the fact. Yet something about the strange old fellow stopped him.

The old man straightened himself importantly, brushing clouds of dust from his clothes and beard. Then, from out of his robe, he pulled a large hourglass.

'Hmmm,' he said. 'Fourteen hundred years have I slept. Now is the time to find the King.'

Arty felt a little concerned for the old gentleman now. He was clearly a bit loopy, and if he went wandering the countryside like this, he could hurt himself. Mr. Jenkins would know what to do.

'Oh . . . yes . . . the King,' said Arty, thinking quickly. 'Perhaps I could help you find him?'

Immediately, the whiskery face lit up. 'Good lad! I could use a guide in this new age. Let us be away!' Merlin raised his arms and there was a blinding FLASH.

Suddenly, Arty was looking at mountains! He knew he was nowhere near Carmarthen now.

'You really are Merlin the wizard!' gasped Arty.

'Of course, boy. King Arthur has returned to heal the land, and I have awoken to join him.'

'Wicked!'

'No. 'Tis most definitely a very good thing,' said Merlin, looking sideways at Arty.

The wizard clicked his fingers and a large map appeared, which hovered in the air.

'Wow!' exclaimed Arty. The map showed the whole of Wales, and at the top it said 'Magick Playses'. A sparkling light showed that they were now right up in Snowdonia.

'Ah, here is the lair,' said Merlin, tapping some boulders with his staff. The large rocks rumbled apart to reveal the entrance to a cave.

'Did you say "lair"?' said Arty in alarm, as he followed Merlin into the darkness.

Then, as Arty's eyes grew accustomed to the gloom, he started to make out a large shape, a shape that was snuffling his ear! When Merlin conjured up a light, Arty's jaw dropped. Before him was an immense red dragon.

'No other dragon is as decent as my wise old friend here,' said Merlin. 'Though, he was fighting a big white dragon when we met, and I was about your age too.'

The wizard greeted the dragon warmly, and took a seat next to its smoking snout. The two talked for a while of old times, but all Arty could do was stand rigid against the cave wall, staring goggle-eyed at the huge beast. Two things were bothering him; what did dragons eat, and was it feeding time?

Merlin at last asked the dragon about the King.

'I can tell you only that for news of Arthur, ask the Twrch Trwyth,' advised the dragon with a rumble.

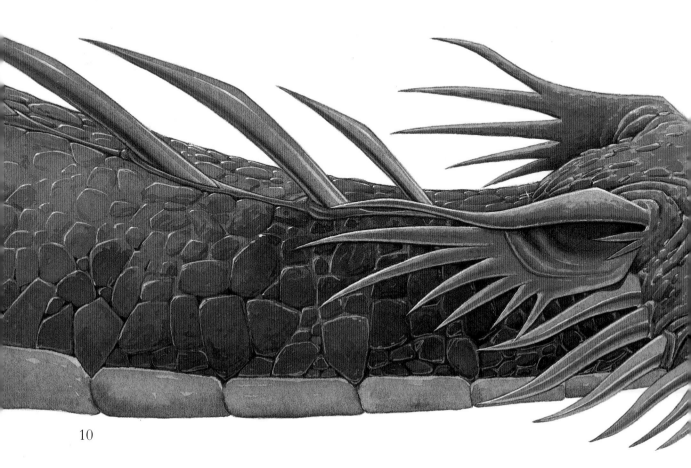

A short while later, and to Arty's great relief, they were standing alive, and in one piece, outside the cave.

Merlin consulted the map.

'Where do you find a Twrch Trwyth?' enquired Arty, still shaking slightly.

'There,' said Merlin, pointing to the Preseli hills on the map. And quick as a FLASH they were standing in a cool, dark wood.

Crashing towards them through the trees came a very large and scruffy wild boar. His ferocious red eyes glared angrily at Arty.

'Don't worry, lad,' reassured Merlin. 'He is no danger to us.'

'Ah, Master Twrch Trwyth,' said Merlin to the great beast, 'we are looking for Arthur. Have you seen him?'

'Raaargh!' roared the monster as it charged.

'Aaaargh!' screamed Merlin and Arty as they ran. Like a shot, they scrambled up the nearest tree.

'I never want to see him again!' the boar called up at them. 'I've not looked my best since that crook took my hairdressing kit.' He turned to stomp huffily away. 'I might have helped you if you'd brought my comb, scissors and razor back,' he growled over his shoulder. Then he disappeared into the greenery.

Gingerly, Arty and the old man climbed down from the tree.
On a road nearby, a milk tanker roared past, making Merlin jump.

'Dragon!' he shouted. 'I can smell its foul breath!'

Above them, jets left vapour trails in the sky as they flew to and
from America. 'They are everywhere!' said Merlin, looking up in
horror.

To calm Merlin down, Arty explained about lorries and planes. He
also told him about the problems of pollution and of global warming;
things he cared about very much.

'I've got ideas to fix everything, though,' he went on. 'I'll invent an engine that runs on water, I'll get people to stop fighting each oth . . .'

He was interrupted by the strange sight of a tiny man running quickly away through the trees.

'Ah, yes,' said Merlin, who had also noticed the little figure. 'The folk of the stones may be of more help than that old boar.' And Merlin led the way up towards a great cromlech.

Suddenly they were surrounded by a crowd of fairies, the Tylwyth Teg. Arty stood amazed as the little people pulled playfully at his clothes.

They were clearly delighted to see Merlin. They flew and danced, laughing and spinning excitedly around them both. Only when they had settled down could Merlin ask them about King Arthur.

'He is not a Man now,' they sang. 'He is one of the Little People!'

'Ah,' said Merlin, clearly disappointed.

As they left them, Arty waved back at the fairy folk, still spinning and laughing around the ancient stones.

'I should have known better than to ask them,' complained Merlin, now quite dejected. 'They're even less help than that boar.'

'The boar might help if we got his hairdressing kit back for him,' said Arty. Merlin looked at him, and frowned. There was a long silence.

'I warn you, it is with the guardian of the Thirteen Treasures of Britain.' He pointed to Bardsey Island on his map.

'So?' asked Arty. There was a FLASH.

17

'He is an extremely large and very grumpy giant,' said Merlin, as he knocked on an enormous wooden door. Arty gulped.

The door opened and Merlin led the way through several halls held up by gigantic pillars. At last they came into a huge, dimly-lit chamber, and Arty found himself looking up at the largest man he had ever seen. The giant was yanking on his beard with a very small comb, mumbling angrily to himself.

'Greetings, mighty Ysbaddaden, Chief of the Giants!' shouted Merlin.

'What do you want, Merlin? My daughter Olwen's calling with the kids today. I've got to look my best, and this fiddly little comb is making me very, very angry! AND WHO'S THIS BOY?' bellowed the giant.

Asking for the hairdressing kit right now seemed a very bad idea. For once, Merlin seemed lost for words.

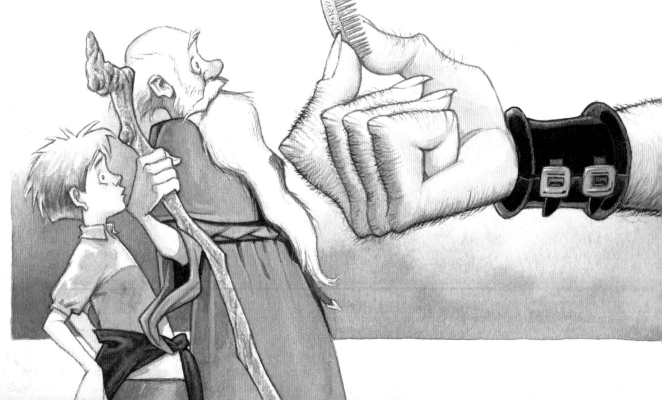

'Great Ysbaddaden,' Arty blurted out, 'I am the humble assistant of the wise and powerful wizard Merlin, who brings you the fabulous Fourteenth Treasure of Britain.'

Merlin stared at Arty, wide-eyed.

'What treasure is that?' said Merlin and Ysbaddaden together.

'The Marvellous Giant Grooming Devices of Picton Terrace,' announced Arty.

'Show me,' said the giant eagerly.

Arty took the puzzled Merlin to one side, and whispered in his ear.

Instantly, there appeared in the middle of the hall Arty's dad's old lawnmower, a pair of rusty shears, and a battered garden rake.

'Wondrous!' said Ysbaddaden as he ran the lawnmower over his head. Great tufts of hair fell to the floor. He raked his long beard gleefully. 'Olwen *will* be pleased. These are much better than the boar's hairdressing kit!' he roared.

'Then we'll take that off your hands,' Arty said quickly. Ysbaddaden, mowing a bald patch across his head, handed it over happily.

When they were at last outside, Merlin turned to Arty in amazement. 'You are a genius, lad!' said the old wizard, and gave Arty a big hug. 'Now to revisit the boar.'

In a FLASH they were back in the shady Preseli woods.

When Arty gave the Twrch Trwyth his razor, scissors and comb, the great boar was overjoyed.

'*Try to see beyond this Age, and Arthur shall be at your side,*' said the boar to Merlin. Then he trotted off into the woods, laughing loudly to himself.

Arty and Merlin were speechless with disappointment. They had gone to all that trouble to get his hairdressing kit back, and now the boar was no help at all! Merlin stared glumly ahead for a very long time. Then, slowly, he turned to Arty.

'*You* are Arthur,' he said in almost a whisper.

'Yeah, that's my proper name,' said Arthur, chewing on a blade of grass.

Merlin sprang up in excitement. 'Arthur the King! Of course, I must have been half asleep not to see it. Not a man, but a little person. Ignore your age, and here you are at my side! Silly me, I've awoken too early!'

Arty sat, stunned.

In a FLASH, they were standing beside a beautiful calm stretch of water. Merlin's map said Bosherston Ponds. Rising out of the water was a glowing arm and in its hand, Arty could make out a small, golden book.

A wooden boat on the bank seemed to be waiting for them. Arty got in with Merlin and together they floated out towards the arm.

'Take the book, Arthur,' urged Merlin.

Arty took it, turned it over in his hands and read the title glowing on the cover; *Everything A Hero Needs To Know.*

'Oh . . . how useful,' said Arty, who really would have preferred a sword.

'Big swords don't change the world, Arthur,' said Merlin, knowing Arty's thoughts. 'Big ideas do that.'

Arty's head bumped back against the stone. He was on the hill outside Carmarthen. His watch said two minutes past ten!

'I must have been dreaming,' he said, rubbing the back of his head.

He looked down at the golden book glowing in his hand. He opened it and read the first page:

**Not everyone is a hero
But anyone can become one**

Arty knew then what he had to do. He crawled out from his hiding place and marched straight to where Morgan was peering into a bush. Arty tapped him sharply on the shoulder, and Morgan spun round in surprise.

'Listen Morgan;' said Arty, inches from Morgan's face. 'I've been sniffed at by a dragon, chased by a giant boar, and shouted at by a very irate giant. You don't scare me, so don't waste my time.'

'Wh . . . wha . . .' stammered Morgan.

'And call me Arthur!' he said, as he turned and marched away.

Arthur made his way up to the very top of the hill and looked down on the winding river below. But where was Merlin now? He opened the book and read the answer:

Merlin has gone for a short nap
— Back in ten years.

Arthur smiled. He couldn't wait.

In his crystal cave, Merlin pulled the sheets up under his chin. As he lay there, he couldn't resist taking just one sneaky peak into the future. Before him appeared a marvellous vision – of new heroes, changing the world and making new legends.

Merlin chuckled quietly to himself and closed his eyes. Still smiling, he started to snore.

Not The End

Magick playses

MAGICAL PLACES

Merlin's Hill

Merlin's Hill is just two miles outside Carmarthen, where Merlin was born. Under the hill Merlin is said to lie asleep in a crystal cave until the day when he will return to help Arthur heal the land. A large stone, shaped like a seat, is hidden somewhere on the hill. Sitting on this stone, Merlin spoke his wise words and foretold the future.

Dinas Emrys

King Vortigen tried to build his fortress here, but the foundations would not hold and the walls kept falling down.

The king's wisest advisors could not help, so the young Merlin was summoned. He revealed that two dragons were fighting in a lake under the hill and they were shaking the building to the ground. The dragons were released, and the red dragon (representing Wales) defeated the white dragon (representing the Saxons).

Pembrokeshire

King Arthur and his knights chased the magic boar, the Twrch Trwyth, all over Pembrokeshire, from the coast to the mountains. This was all because Arthur's cousin Culhwch loved Olwen, daughter of Ysbaddaden, chief of the giants. The giant gave Culhwch the task of getting for him the scissors, comb and razor belonging to the Twrch Trwyth before he would let Culhwch marry Olwen.

Pentre Ifan

The cromlech has been standing here for over five thousand years. Legend says that fairies are sometimes seen around the ancient stones. The woods nearby are thought to have been a sacred place of the druids.

Bardsey Island

Known in Welsh as Ynys Enlli, the island is said by some to be the Isle of Avalon. The thirteen magical treasures of Britain are hidden here.

Bosherston

It is said that the Lily Ponds are where Excalibur was returned to the Lady of the Lake after Arthur's final battle. The ponds were actually only created in the 18th-19th century, but nearby in a small hidden valley is a pool that is much older.

There are magical places all over Wales; these are just a few of them.
Others can still be found today, and are written about in other books.

For Joseff and Jacob

The author gratefully acknowledges the help
of Mr and Mrs Richards of the Merlin's Hill
Centre, Abergwili, and the National Trust at
Stackpole and Dinas Emrys.

First Impression – 2003
Second Impression – 2004

ISBN 1 84323 211 1

This title is published with the support of the
Arts Council of Wales.

Printed in Wales at
Gomer Press, Llandysul, Ceredigion